koala

TEDDY BEAR
Honorary 'Bear'
Worldwide

The Teddy bear is a stuffed
toy bear named after the US
president Theodore Roosevelt
whose nickname was Teddy.

BROWN BEAR
Ursus arctos
Europe, Asia and North America

Brown bears are the most common
of all bears. They can be found all
over North America, Europe
and Asia.

SUN BEAR
Helarctos malayanus
Southeast Asia

The sun bear is the world's
smallest bear. The sun bear is also
known as a honey bear because it
loves to eat honey.

For Emily and Jessica

First published by Fremantle Press, Australia, in 2010.

Published in the United States of America in 2013 by Star Bright Books. Inc.
The name Star Bright Books and the Star Bright Books logo are registered
trademarks of Star Bright Books, Inc. Please visit: www.starbrightbooks.com.
For bulk orders, please email: orders@starbrightbooks.com, or call customer
service at: (617) 354-1300.

Hardback ISBN-13: 978-1-59572-638-4
Star Bright Books / MA / 00107130
Printed in China (C&C) 10 9 8 7 6 5 4 3 2 1

Paperback ISBN-13: 978-1-59572-639-1
Star Bright Books / MA / 00107130
Printed in China (C&C) 10 9 8 7 6 5 4 3 2 1

Library of Congress Cataloging-in-Publication Data

Thompson, Michael, 1977- author, illustrator.
 The other bears / written and illustrated by Michael Thompson.
     pages cm
 "First published by Fremantle Press, Australia, in 2010."
 Summary: "Mother and Father Koala are suspicious of the 'other' bears.
They don't like the panda bears and they don't trust the polar bears.
But their grumpiness melts away as they watch their little Koalas play
together with 'other' bears"-- Provided by publisher.
 ISBN 978-1-59572-638-4 (hardcover) -- ISBN 978-1-59572-639-1 (pbk.)
 [1. Koala--Fiction. 2. Bears--Fiction. 3. Toleration--Fiction.] I. Title.
 PZ7.T37195Ot 2013
 [E]--dc23
                              2012036956

The Other Bears

By Michael Thompson

Star Bright Books
Cambridge, Massachusetts

Koalas just LOVE to
be called koala bears.

But they were in for a big surprise

when the *other* bears arrived.

First came the panda bears.

"I don't like their ears," grumbled Father Koala.

"Or their shoes," griped Mother Koala.

"But we love their food," grinned the little koalas.

Next came the polar bears.

"I don't like their claws," growled Father Koala.

"Or their coats," groaned Mother Koala.

"But we love their jokes," giggled the little koalas.

Third came the black bears.

"I don't like their noise," wailed Father Koala.

"Or their uniforms," whined Mother Koala.

"But we love their songs," whooped the little koalas.

Then came the brown bears.

"I don't like their teeth," snapped Father Koala.

"Or that hat," sniffed Mother Koala.

"But we love their stories," said the little koalas.

Last came the sun bears.

"I don't like their bicycles," huffed Father Koala.

"Or their umbrellas," puffed Mother Koala.

"But we love their games," laughed the little koalas.

Father Koala and Mother Koala

were becoming so grumpy

they didn't seem to like anything anymore.

But then . . .

All their grumpiness melted away,

watching the little koalas play.

For each was a happier little bear,

now that the other bears were there.

KOALA
Phascolarctos cinereus
Eastern and Southern Australia

Koalas are not really bears. They are
marsupials, animals that carry their babies in
a pouch. Koalas eat mostly eucalyptus leaves,
and they sleep for about 16 hours a day.